Finding Lily

Elizabeth Goddard

Finding Lily

This edition is published by
That Guy's House in 2017

www.ThatGuysHouse.com

Finding Lily

Finding Lily

This is the story of
Love
Loss
Trauma
Healing
and Forgiveness

This is the story of finding the Diamond

This is dedicated to you the reader
This is dedicated to you the seeker
This is dedicated to you the diamond

...

and this is dedicated to Lily

Elizabeth Goddard

Welcome
to
my
book.

Finding Lily

On the 12th and 13th of April 2014 I attended a Psychic Art workshop in London hosted by Roger Hanson of rogerhansonlove.com.

One of the exercises we were shown was how to use art to heal emotions and as I did this, an event from my past came forward, along with a lot of tears, as I felt the pain I had locked away for many years.

As the memory came forward and it was totally unexpected, I found myself drawing a red heart. As I dropped in further to the event I started to colour out my emotions and when I had finished the heart was gone and I had a black sheet.

The cover of this book is a re-creation of that original artwork, but instead of pain I drew this with love...

Liz Goddard
22nd June 2017

Elizabeth Goddard

Finding Lily

The Creator gathered all of Creation and said, "I want to hide something from humans until they are ready for it. It's the realisation that they create their own reality".

The Eagle said, "Give it to me. I will take it to the moon".
The Creator said, "No. One day they will go there and find it".

The Salmon said, "I will bury it on the bottom of the ocean".
The Creator said, "No. One day they will go there too".

The Buffalo said, "I will bury it on the Great Plains".
The Creator said, "They will cut into the skin of the Earth and find it even there".

Grandmother Mole who lives in the breast of Mother Earth and who has no physical eyes but sees with spiritual eyes said,

"Put it inside of them".
And the Creator said "It is done".

- HOPI CREATION STORY

Elizabeth Goddard

Forward

This is my story, told, as I remember it… I have written it as fiction, but it is based on actual events.

When I decided to write the book, the idea was to start to break open the taboo of abortion, and, I still do want to do that.

I am a Soul Purpose Coach helping women through big transitions - Healing the past for a clearer brighter future. I believe we are all working on ourselves constantly, evolving, continuously. I've studied massage and reflexology and worked in spas and for myself.

I started to wake up spiritually when my daughter was born in 1993 and she continues to be a guiding light for me.

Elizabeth Goddard

I had ignored the signs before that, when I was growing up I found I didn't fit in easily and I certainly didn't want to stand out…

I was brought up in a Catholic household, attended church every Sunday and went to a Catholic School. I was torn between what I had been told was right and wrong (which I didn't believe) and what my gut was telling me what was right.

When my daughter was born, she cried constantly, literally 24 hours a day. I knew this wasn't right, I spoke to my doctor who told me just to leave her to cry, but as a parent you know the difference between tiredness and hunger, this was pain.

When she was nearly two I read a letter in a magazine, it was thanking them for an article and in the letter they described my daughter exactly. I called the telephone number the following day and managed to get an emergency appointment, they could hear her in the background crying and fitted us in. The letter, phone call and appointment changed our lives!

The day following the appointment I stood in awe in the kitchen watching my child become a different person, she was happy and laughing.

I was amazed at the transformation and this started me on the road to understanding how we can heal ourselves with help (it was not instant; it has taken me a long time to fit it all together). How the answer isn't in a bottle and that doctors don't always know best.

Finding Lily

Over the next couple of years, I was promoted a few times at work, my children were between the ages of 13 and 4, and I was working full-time and running a household single handlily. I contacted a Kinesiologist to help me with my stress levels and this led me to have a healing crisis.

I was signed off from work for 3 weeks and within 6 weeks I had handed in my notice at work, signed up for an Indian Head Massage course and whilst waiting to join that found myself on a Reiki course. When something is meant to happen, it does, that was in 1999!
My life changed in so many ways, the life I existed in disintegrated and I emerged stronger and more empowered.

I thought I was sorted, I thought I had dealt with the trauma of my past.

Following my training, in 1999 through to 2001, I was changing. Sadly my husband at the time wasn't and it saw the breakup of our marriage. I continued to work as a therapist but, supporting three young children on my own, I needed to go back to work that fitted in with their needs; I ended up back in sales where I started many years ago.
After a few years there, I started to help someone who was dealing with the death of his sister. One conversation led me to look in to life coaching, and once again my life started to change.

Elizabeth Goddard

I went on to train with Blue Marsden at the Holistic Healing College as a Spiritual Life Coach, Soul Plan Practitioner and Theta Healer. I started working more in this area working with people aligning themselves. I also started working more helping people with empowerment and limiting beliefs.

In April 2016 I went on the Core Issue therapy - Soul Transformation course in Hastings with Blue.
I knew it would be a perfect fit with the Soul Plan, as it uses the same energies. I found it actually linked in with a therapy I had learned in 2002 called Past Life Energetics and one of the techniques I have been incorporating in to my sessions with clients.

For me personally, I found I was able to use Core Issue Therapy for myself, something I wasn't able to do with the Past Life Energetics. And as we are here to fix ourselves, it has been perfect.

In the May, I used the Core Issue Therapy for myself and did a Soul Retrieval and this book has stemmed from that one healing session.
It shocked me, and rocked me at the time, but it linked perfectly with work I have been interested in.

It was very powerful and I felt it was putting me back together fully again. What happened in the session wasn't a soul retrieval but a reclaiming of a part of me that escaped to protect herself. When I write my blogs and newsletters I talk about us all being a work in progress, constantly evolving and growing.

Following that healing I decided to write this story, but as it emerged over the pages, it seemed to become more about forgiveness and reclaiming my self; finding my diamond. I realised that I had spent time healing the hurt and anger I felt personally, but I never realised I needed to heal the events that surrounded it.

In 2012 I had attended a workshop in London and I was shocked when the abortion came up, I had thought of it often in the first 5 or so years, and then yearly on the anniversary. During the weekend I managed to release and forgive myself for the event, but the anger and hurt that got me to that point had been left hanging. In fact I don't even think I acknowledged them.

I had an abortion at the age of 26, and by reading the story you will understand why. I couldn't ask for help, I daren't ask for help, I was in a bubble and I didn't really get that, until now.

This event had been pushed into a box for 22 years before it finally made its appearance, I hid it away, never spoke about it, but I did think about it. Initially I thought about it a lot, as the years passed, and on certain dates the sorrow would come back.

I needed to mentally cope with that decision and what I went through at the time. But it wasn't until I started tapping at the keys I realised there was more healing to be done.

This isn't just for anyone who has had an abortion, it is for anyone who needs to forgive and forgive on all levels.

And it is about allowing to let go.

At the end, I have added two healing practices for you, if that is what you need.

I had no intention of writing this book, I have, in fact, been compiling information for another one over the last 2 years, this came out of the blue.

When we experience any form of trauma, parts of ourselves can breakaway to protect us and stay whole and undamaged. But, what can happen is they never reintegrate with us, they stay where they are.

What happened, and what I learnt, I am working on now as a new healing modality, so out of the pain is coming something beautiful.

I have never hidden to anyone that I am constantly trying to clear and heal, I believe we all have something to deal with and this is our journey. I also believe this is the time for us to deal with the trauma and issues that have come through our DNA.

Finding Lily

I have been on a personal journey; I still am on one, trying to find out the best way to deal with this. This is the time to let go of any little speck still in me relating to that time, holding me back.

I was working with Kerry Rowlett of Awaken Kinesiology for my business and she gave me an affirmation in the December of 2015, linked to Monkey Flower Essence:

I welcome awareness of my attitudes.
Easily and simply I now release in to unconditional love my conditioned tendency towards: feeling ashamed of my needs, deep vulnerability about what I see as my own inadequacies, inability to open up to others about myself for fear of exposure.
I accept the challenge to reveal myself without shame.
I recognise this moment of change welcoming my commitment to work through my feelings of shame, guilt, unworthiness and the fear of exposure and rejection with a safe person.

I repeated this daily.

This was quite big for me, as when I first was given it, I couldn't say the words; some of them wouldn't come out of my mouth, some of the sentences were jumbled. When I went to check the date I got this; I found a message telling her that it took me 8-9 times before the words would come out. I believe this was also coming up for me, helping me work through the feelings of shame, guilt and unworthiness.

I have also looked at the effect it has had on relationships following this time, including my children, particularly my son.

I don't want to pretend it didn't happen, it did, I needed to make myself whole.

I want to shine like a diamond!

'There is complete
silence around her, but I can
feel her heart breaking. It is
being cracked open and I
can hear a silent sobbing
coming from deep inside
her, but for an outsider you
wouldn't know that, *you*
can't hear it.

Finding Lily

Elizabeth Goddard

Elizabeth Goddard

Finding the Diamond

"Oh Crap"

I look around the cafe and it is full!

Just like being at home...

All I need is a few minutes thinking space, well not
evening thinking space, 'non' thinking space. My
head is about to explode! I have so many titles, and
people I answer to. I have so many projects I want
to complete and so many ideas running round my
head.

I need just a few minutes, without someone needing
something from me.

"It's hot in here as well! Why has every man and his
dog decided to come here at the same time as me?"

Finding Lily

As I order my tea, I look around for a table that I can share; a space I can sit without having to speak to anyone.

Scanning the cafe I notice a table outside, there is a girl sitting by herself, "brilliant" and she looks like she wants to be left alone as well.

Don't get me wrong, I love my job, I love working and helping my clients, I adore my family, but sometimes you need a clear head to think through new ideas. You do need to get out somewhere else.

Just sit and watch, just be…

Maybe I should have gone for a walk instead…

Why did I think it was going to be quiet here? It is always busy.

How the fuck did I get to this point, where I just need out? I never used to be like this.

Grabbing my tea, I walk outside towards her and I indicate to the empty chair, she barely lifts her head, she half nods so I sit down.
I used to love spending time with people, it's really weird.

Elizabeth Goddard

I rummage in my bag for my journal and place it on the table, hopefully that way people won't disturb me.

It sometimes works, it often doesn't; I must have one of those faces.

People must see me deep in thought, or working, but they still start talking to me. I really need to start working on my boundaries; I find it rude to ignore them. Even when I just look up and smile and look down again they still keep talking at me. I wonder why that is? It's like when complete strangers tell me their life stories on the train or a queue in the supermarket, I just can't stop them.

Anyway this is my time - TFM, 'time for me' as someone I used work with called it.

I glance up at the girl and I sense a sadness around her, one that I recognise.

That's the problem with being an empath, you feel others emotions and pain…

It's a knowing; you know something is wrong or you can feel something isn't quite right.

Finding Lily

I can't quite remember when it started, I think I must have always had it, but not been aware or tuned in to it.

I can remember when I really started to notice it, the alarm clock radio came on one morning and I was half listening to the DJs, and remember thinking that's odd, he has split up from his wife. Then a few months later it came out that he had. It happened again a while later with the same show and I got the same feeling, and the main DJ had as well.

Stop, stop, stop; I have come here to clear my head not bog it down with more thoughts.

TFM!

I look at her again and then look around, I bet no one else has even noticed her hiding away in the corner. Her long dark hair, pulled back fiercely in a ponytail, her big sad eyes, so full of sorrow and pain. I bet they have all walked passed her, or avoided her, but, for some reason I was drawn to her.

I feel the pain that is emanating from her.

I look away again, I really need to clear my head; this is my time now. Free for a while, I could just sit here all day, no one would know. I could turn my phone

off, I have nothing urgent to deal with today; I just
need some space.

When you have so many people in your life you
need to take time out; that's what I teach my clients,
but I seem to have gotten out of the habit of
booking time out for me. I don't seem to get much
time to do it myself at the moment,

I am going to have to change that. I will do this now
a few times a week. I will clear an hour out of my
diary and come here for a coffee or take myself to
breakfast, at that little place in Gomshall; time just
for me. When I did it a few months ago it was pure
bliss, I need more of that!

"Oh God!". There she goes again, that pain!

There is complete silence around her, but I can feel
her heart breaking. It is being cracked open and I
can hear a silent sobbing coming from deep inside
her, but for an outsider you wouldn't know that, you
can't her it.

There is no sign on her face, there isn't a sound
coming from her, but I can feel it. I can feel her
crying from a place deep within. There is a blank
distant look, she could almost be dead; there is
nothing in her eyes. I have never experienced

picking up anything like this before; there was one client who had been through a violent relationship, and I felt that, I could feel trauma of her being thrown against a wall, but this is different, that was a flashback and pain, this is pure emotion.

As I look away, I know that feeling, I remember it only too well. It is as if I am sitting watching myself age 26, my heart is breaking, but I think I would have been more vocal. Perhaps not then, I would be now. I suffered a lot in silence, a lot then.

"Oh My God" there it is again, what do I do?

Do I say something to her?

She will think I'm nuts if I say "I feel your pain".

If someone had said that to me what would I have done?

She may think who is this crazy woman... Maybe I am a crazy woman…

Maybe, I'm in a parallel universe and it is me sitting opposite me; watching me.

Maybe, this is one of those moments where I get to go back in time and tell myself it is all going to be

Elizabeth Goddard

ok. Like writing a letter to the younger you, one of those empowerment exercises - what would you tell the younger you?

What would I tell the younger me?

"It will all be fine, if you could see your life now, you have to go through this", I would leave all the crap out that has happened in between "you have two more beautiful children and you have a grandson. You have changed your career a few times and been really successful each time".

But this cafe wasn't here, then, when I was 26, I think it was a toy shop, it has only been a cafe for couple of years, if that.

Maybe that is just part of the experience.

"Shit" this emotion is taking me back to another lifetime, a lifetime I thought I had dealt with.
I know I have dealt with it, I spent a lot of time, four years ago, dealing with the trauma.

Or have I?

I look up at her again, I must stop looking at her, she will wonder what I am doing, her body is there, but her soul is missing.

Finding Lily

Bless her, I know what is it like to feel like that, her story maybe different, but the emotion is the same.

How can I still be coming back to this trauma 26 years later?

Maybe I am supposed to be here, maybe the need to clear my head today is partly to be here with her.

Maybe, I need to feel her pain in order to heal the part of me that got left behind. Maybe, it is time to re-integrate that 26 year old that got left behind.

That's a lot of maybes...

"God", I remember that feeling, trying to pretend everything is OK, when in reality it is not.

Finding Lily

Elizabeth Goddard

Life Just Goes On

I find it amazing how life just goes on around you, when you are grieving for someone or something. It's like losing someone close, a friend or family member or even a pet. I remember when my Grandfather died and thinking why is everyone so happy, can't you see I am in pain! Shut the fuck up!

All around us there are people chatting and laughing why can't they feel the emotion and sorrow crying out from this young girl?
She may be a woman, it is hard to tell with that vacant look. I want to scream for her "can't you feel she is in pain".

As I look across the road, over to the lush green grass on the village cricket pitch, in this gorgeous little village, I realise how far I have actually come.

Maybe I had to live the same pain as her, to get here to this moment.

Elizabeth Goddard

Do I say anything to her?
Will I make it worse?
What if I let her know I am here if she wants to talk?

How?

I look up again and she is there, a bit more present,
something coming alive in her eyes. Maybe she has
heard me screaming internally at everyone around
us.

I smile, I don't really know what else to do, and I see
her mouth move ever so slightly in an attempt to
smile back.

"God", I remember that feeling, trying to pretend
everything is OK, when in reality it is not.

When you are in a situation like that you get consumed, you can't think clearly, shock, grief, fear what ever the emotion or emotions coming up can stem the rational clear thinking you.

Finding Lily

Elizabeth Goddard

Elizabeth Goddard

It's funny the odd moments you recall…

I remember coming out of a Sainsburys cafe and getting in to my car. I remember clearly taking a call from my doctor.

I was single; a single mother and pregnant, I had been to see her about a termination, she said she would see if she could arrange it for me, and she called to tell me she couldn't.

Another "maybe" coming.

Maybe I should have taken it as a sign, a sign that I should keep this child, but I didn't.

I remember thinking what am I going to do now? I know now, 26 years later, I would have seen it as a sign, or would I have taken notice being in that situation? When you are in a situation like that you get consumed, you can't think clearly, shock, grief, fear what ever the emotion or emotions coming up can stem the rational clear thinking you. Clouding your

Finding Lily

thought process, well it is for me. I find myself drifting off in to nowhere, staring into space without the capacity to think.

I was going to have to tell my ex-partner, he wanted me to have the abortion.

I don't actually remember how I felt about it at that point, I think I was just numb, I was probably still in shock. Shock I was pregnant and shock that he didn't want the baby.

I was able to do the everyday stuff, but it wasn't me doing them, it was like an out of body experience. It was if I was standing next to me watching me, a bit like now, watching this girl sat next to me.

I just went along with his wishes and I don't think I even thought there was another way.

It never occurred to me that I was already bringing up one child, so I had the knowledge. The situation would be different but I had the experience. I am sure I could have figured something out given the chance. Perhaps rejection played a large part of it.

I was now going to have to tell him, he was going to have to find the money, I didn't have it. I think looking back there was a naive part of me that wished he couldn't afford it and I could then keep the baby. Other forces were at work, and for him this one was fear.

I inwardly chuckle as someone opens the cafe door and Paloma Faith-Picking Up The Pieces is playing in the background.

Finding Lily

Elizabeth Goddard

The Domino Effect

But, the pain I am feeling now, this one that I recognise feeling many, many years ago. The pain coming from this girl didn't come from that moment, it was from a series of events leading up to that point.

Some events I had no idea about, these would come later. I was just going along in a bubble, doing what I was told was the best for me...

26 years later and after collecting most of the puzzle pieces, I was able to put it all together.

Only I didn't quite get them all, some are still missing; it's like having a puzzle and on the front of the box, it says this is a 500 piece puzzle but counting them you only have 495. You know, if you made it, you would still be able to work out what the picture was though.

Elizabeth Goddard

Maybe now is the time to create that picture.

I inwardly chuckle as someone opens the cafe door and Paloma Faith- Picking Up The Pieces is playing in the background.

Maybe this is the time to finally heal everything, not just the bits I have been doing individually.

It is as if my brain has recorded a snapshot, a bit leading up and a bit afterwards, magically everything has been protected or I have been protected.

Finding Lily

Elizabeth Goddard

Elizabeth Goddard

Picking up the pieces

It is funny how you remember some things and not others. I was in Sainsburys, Crawley and before the phone call, I had eaten a jacket potato as I was so hungry and it helped with the sickness, I don't remember the topping.

I do remember reading in the Daily Mail, something about Tony Blair, I can't remember if he had just got in, timing wasn't right for an election, but he was the new best thing, perhaps he was the new leader of the Labour Party, does it really matter?
No, it doesn't really, but out of all that was happening, I remember it clearly. It is as if my brain has recorded a snapshot, a bit leading up and a bit afterwards, magically everything has been protected or I have been protected.
And if I went back there now I could point out exactly where I was sitting. That is the last time I ever went there, I must have found somewhere else to call in for a coffee or a snack.

Finding Lily

After the call, I have no idea what I did or where I went. I was in field sales, I don't know if I continued with my sales calls that afternoon. I don't know if I called the father to tell him or waited until I saw him later that evening, we were still living together, but sleeping in separate rooms now. This was what he wanted, not me, and I do remember there being an anger around it as well. He was angry and agitated, and I didn't understand why.

I had a 5 year old son and I loved being a mother and wanted more children.

This wasn't what the 7 year old me had dreamed of when playing with my dolls. I can't even recall how I felt, I don't think I cried in the car, this was the time before mobiles, I had a car phone, the mobiles weren't really mobile, you had a battery the size of a breeze block which if I recall the handset attached to it. Then, a mobile phone was larger than your average handbag. I think my brother-in-law still has one in the loft.

It wouldn't be for another few months until I found out why all this was happening to me.

I think I was at this point because of one night; I think I can pin point the event that would change this part of my life. The piece I pull out and lay down first.

Finding Lily

Elizabeth Goddard

Thirteen months Earlier

I looked back again and the girl is still there, staring ahead. I gaze back in the direction she is staring, I now have most of the pieces in front of me and I start looking at them.

I think I was at this point because of one night; I think I can pin point the event that would change this part of my life. The piece I pull out and lay down first.

This one is from 13 months earlier.

We were living together and we worked together on the sales team. It was December, and as a Team we went out to celebrate Christmas. It is the first time I really remember all of us going out and some of the directors joining us. We were at the Rum Wong in Guildford, we were all sat on cushions on the floor eating our meal. I noticed my partner, who was sitting a couple of cushions along from me falling backwards, being pushed with great hilarity by one of our colleagues, I thought nothing of it, I was quite secure in our relationship.

Elizabeth Goddard

We had been living together for quite a while, the three of us, which included my son, he was from a previous relationship.

How wrong was I?

As the evening went on, we made our way down in to the town to a nightclub, where someone made a pass at me, had he seen more than I had with them? Or maybe it had been going on a while. At this point now, I don't really need to know, it really is irrelevant to me, at the time it wouldn't have been.

What I do know was I was horrified at this pass.

After a few hours and a few more drinks we all made our way to get taxis, I got in the first one but he didn't. There were too many people, so he stayed back with the colleague who had been pushing him earlier and said they would get another, I don't remember if it was just the two of them or anyone else was with them.
What I do remember was that one of the guys was sick on the way back to Woking, when we got to our house, we had to clean the taxi for the driver. So I have no idea how long it was before they turned up, they could have been following us or it could have been an hour later.

But what I do know is that it was around this time their relationship started. And this event, for me, was like the first domino and was about to knock all the pieces over...

Numbness is a feeling I know well. It is a non feeling, a way of coping and that is how I coped by not feeling. This has never left me, I do a lot of things not to feel…
Mainly with wine.

Finding Lily

Elizabeth Goddard

Elizabeth Goddard

Numbness is a feeling
I know well.

*When I walked out of the coffee shop at Sainsbury's and took
the call from my doctor, I had no idea this was the reason I
was terminating the pregnancy.*

*It was really to protect him from being caught having an
affair. And, being caught having an affair with the woman he
had cheated on me with in the first place. AND, at this point
I didn't even know he had been cheating or that he was seeing
her. I thought he was still as single as me, living in the same
house as me.*

I look back at the girl, she is still there, I can feel a
numbness coming from her, a void.

Numbness is a feeling I know well. It is a non
feeling, a way of coping and that is how I coped by

not feeling. This has never left me, I do a lot of
things not to feel… Mainly with wine.

I look back over the expanse of the green, the cute
little cottages in a neat row behind it, the cricket hut
slightly to the right. I can hear either the Reading or
Redhill train pulling in to the station.

*I have no idea when I found out when I was pregnant, it must
have been sometime in January.*

*I remember our relationship deteriorating over the months
following that meal and in the September I suggested
separating. I had nowhere really to go so moved in to the spare
room. I had no idea that he was having an affair. The signs
were there if I look back now…*

*I do remember being on a sales course with the team some time
earlier that year and one of the guys I worked with telling me
he had seen them going in to her room. I brushed it off, she
was friends with both of us; they wouldn't do that. She would
often stay over after work on a Friday now; we (she and I)
used to go to an exercise class once a week.*

*Whenever we went away with work my ex and I would be
booked separate rooms even though we were in a relationship
and I do remember him staying with me that night.*

Elizabeth Goddard

Another thing I remember was the trainer turning up hours late the next day, due to an accident on the M4. I remember everyone suffering with hangovers and him walking with her in the morning, he said it was because she had a hangover. Maybe she was upset he hadn't been with her, but I am only surmising. And, although I remember them walking outside of the hotel, it has never occurred to me until now, but why would it...

I know our relationship had been changing over the months leading up to September, I wonder now if part of me thought it was temporary. But I remember our relationship didn't change much more than me sleeping in the spare room. I used to pay rent and I used to buy my own food.

I told one of my bosses we were separating, he agreed it was a good idea, but never said a word. It would appear I was the only one in the company who didn't know what was going on. Even after we separated, not one person said a word or gave me a hint that they were an item.

So that first piece, that first moment they connected, whenever it was November, December, it really doesn't matter to me now, that moment was having a ripple effect on my life, my sons life and the baby living inside of me.

My doctor had given me a number, I must have called it at some point, but I don't remember that. I must have made an appointment. I have no recollection of anything around that time.

What I do remember is my sons 6th birthday and being very distant. I remember he had a caterpillar cake, I have a photo of him grinning but I don't really remember being fully there.

I remember my mum coming over, I think it was a Friday evening, my ex was still at the wine bar I think, my mum suggested getting fish and chips, and I do remember driving past the bar and wondering if he was in there and why he wasn't home with us. I know we weren't together as a couple officially, but we still did things as we had always done. Shopping on a Saturday, popping over to see his mum at the weekend, we were still doing all that, but we were separated. It is funny how you remember those small things and lock the pain away.

I look back at the girl; she is still sat there staring, half there now half not, what is her story? What are her thoughts?

Maybe it is me and my ego thinking I am here to help her heal her pain. She does look slightly familiar.

The hair pulled back fiercely, I would have done that, not wanting people to see me as beautiful, as I didn't deserve it. I would have wanted to fade in to the background.

Today I use that look but as a way of a homemade face lift!

I have no idea how I got here, or what has happened in between. I know it is the afternoon. I have no idea how I managed to get my diary to work when I should be in Sussex.

Finding Lily

Elizabeth Goddard

Elizabeth Goddard

Friday the 14th

I look back out across the green again and I am traveling, it's a bit like the film The Time Traveller's Wife...

It is now two weeks later, it is a Friday; my ex has borrowed the money to pay for the abortion.

I am in Richmond looking for the building, stupidly I think it would be easy to locate, and that there would be a big sign outside...

I have no idea how I got here, or what has happened in between. I know it is the afternoon. I have no idea how I managed to get my diary to work when I should be in Sussex.

But I am here.

Finding Lily

Again, it is only the small things that my brain can recall. I don't remember if I was nervous, I don't recall if we spoke about it or what he would have said.

We still lived in the same house, but I have no idea what we talked about, if anything at all.

Did he wish me well?
Did he understand what I would have been going through?
Was he just feeling relief that he was getting away with not being caught?

I found the road and the anonymous building. I think there was parking to the side of it. Why would I remember that? I remember it as a sort of add-on to the side of the building. I don't remember going in to the main part.

As I said it was a Friday; Friday the 14th of February. Valentines day.

I must have filled out forms in the waiting area, they would have needed some information, I do remember meeting a woman, I don't know if she was a doctor, she must have been. We sat opposite each other with what seemed like a huge desk dividing us. I remember it being a dark room and feeling very small. I remember her asking me questions but I don't recall what they were.

Elizabeth Goddard

I told her that when I fell pregnant, it was over the New Year and I had been out drinking and was worried it would affect the baby. That was the story I was feeding myself. That was my reason for justifying it. This was the lie I was protecting myself with. I was just falling in to line.

She never said "no don't be silly it will be fine", what she did say was I met the criteria and that I needed two medical signatures and was good to go - she didn't say the last bit... She did say that as I had been referred by my doctor I only needed another and she was happy to sign it, so she must have been a doctor.

I do remember something inside of me screaming "No! Stop it! This isn't what I want"! I wanted her to say "I don't think you are doing it for the right reasons"... I remember wanting her to save me from this situation, a reason to go back and say they won't let me...

It is quite childlike in a way, I really needed someone who I could talk to, who could have stood up for me or asked me what I really wanted, it was too late now.

It was like the part of me that had gone in to hiding had finally woken up, but now it was too late.

I wonder how many women get to that appointment and realise they don't want to go through with it, and out of those women how many walk away, I didn't sadly.

Finding Lily

But, there are no mistakes these are just learnings…

What was this young girl sitting next to me doing?
What was she going through?
Did she have a similar story to mine?
Or was her pain from something else?

I get up and go inside and get some water, she was
still there staring out in to space.

Who was she?

What was she going through?

As I sat back down and opened my book again, off I
went again back in to the past.

*I am driving back towards Woking after the appointment, I
have no idea what time it was, I think it was dark. There are
a pile of papers on the passenger seat, all the things I need to
be aware of, what could happen, how I need to be taken care
of in the following days. I was feeling numb again. I remember
pulling over to the petrol station, maybe I got fuel, I know I
bought some cigarettes and then headed back.*

*I don't know if I went in to work all smiles or if I went
straight to the wine bar.*

Elizabeth Goddard

I do remember talking to a friend and getting annoyed when I realised I must have left the cigarettes in the garage; this was the time when you could still smoke inside.

I also remember her bursting in to the bar full of life and energy interrupting our conversation and I also remember my friend firmly telling her "we are talking", I don't think that stopped her, "you are interrupting our conversation" and she moved on to a group of people standing behind him. I was so thankful for that, she did it a lot to me, and to have someone standup for me when I really needed it, had he tuned in to what I was going through?

I remember only the small things not the emotion I was feeling, maybe it was my way of coping.

It never actually occurred to me why she was there that evening; she had lost her job weeks before, back at the very beginning of January, and she lived 60 miles away.

It also never occurred to me why she had been at our house a few weeks earlier on a Monday morning.

I called into the house between leaving the weekly sales meeting and making my way to another meeting, waves of sickness coming over me, I headed back quickly. My ex had the day off. I remember rushing into the kitchen heading to the sink, he met me in the kitchen; seeing her car, I remember asking, "what is 'she' doing here?" I have no idea what he said, I ran upstairs to the bathroom. She never left the lounge to say hello or chat, I never saw her. Again, this part of the puzzle would become clearer later... I must have realised, I can't have been that stupid, maybe I didn't want to know, maybe I just accepted what he told me.

Anyway, back to the 14th, I remember him turning up at the wine bar, I don't remember him really acknowledging me, but I could be wrong, I know he went to the group of people behind us. I remember trying to get his attention and finally telling him that we needed to talk, he said later at home. Not unreasonable as we were out with work colleagues.

I must have left to pick my son up, I don't remember. I must have put him to bed. I must have packed his case as he was off to Devon the next day. How can I have lost a huge chunk of my life?

I remember all the other occasions but not this time. I must have arranged it, but I just don't remember. What I do remember is sitting at home waiting for my ex and I remember feeling very, very alone.

I was still sat at the kitchen table waiting to speak to him when he got back at 11:30. He didn't really seem interested until I told him I wanted to stay in overnight and when I told him it would cost an extra £110.00. I knew that would be like a kick to the balls, he hated parting with money unless it was something for himself. By now I had realised he wasn't going to be there for me in any way, he would pick me up,

Elizabeth Goddard

take me home and cook something. Would he sit with me, would he listen if I needed to talk?

The loneliness is the hardest thing, when you just need someone to put their arms around you.

Is this what the young girl was feeling? Lost and hurt and very alone?

I now realise I seem to be more in tune with my old feelings than what is going on for her.
I can no longer feel the pain coming from her now, I feel only mine, is this part of the journey?
She was still sat there, still lost in thought, but I can't feel her emotion.

There are still people laughing and enjoying the sunshine, why was I here?

When he finally got back, I remember asking him where he had been. He knew I had been to the appointment and I needed to discuss things, he told me he had been for a meal with a couple just the three of them, I asked why they would want him there on Valentines evening, I don't remember what he said.

I remember the pain of being let down, of not having anyone there to support me, it was a big dark black hole, a place of nothingness, I was hiding in this cave of despair and not wanting to do what I was going to do.

Finding Lily

Elizabeth Goddard

Elizabeth Goddard

Saturday 15th February

I turn around and she is still there, but she must have got up at some point and got herself another drink as now she has some water in front of her. Wow, how long had I been sitting here lost in thought?

I remember the pain of being let down, of not having anyone there to support me, it was a big dark black hole, a place of nothingness, I was hiding in this cave of despair and not wanting to do what I was going to do. I have no idea if I slept, the next thing I remember, is being in Richmond again the following morning, showing him where to park. I went in a different door this time, I am sure he must have come in with me to pay, leaving my son in the car.

I do remember sitting in the waiting room on my own. I remember the pain of not being with my son when he left for the week, the first time I hadn't been there. I have no idea what was going through his 6 year old head. I had said goodbye but I felt I was leaving him, maybe part of me was.

This pain is so
unbearable, it is
indescribable, I am
actually feeling it now, my
heart is breaking and my
chest hurts, my eyes fill with
tears. I don't know where it
is coming from, I have never
felt this pain
before. Well I have, once
before…

Finding Lily

Elizabeth Goddard

Elizabeth Goddard

The Black Hole

She is still sitting there, next to me, staring out. Her pain isn't there now though, is she in the void I am feeling, thinking back?

I only remember sitting in the waiting room alone, I don't really remember much else, but if I went there again I'd know where I was sitting. I remember looking around the room and everyone having someone with them, maybe a friend, partner or mother, I was the only one alone. And, that is how I felt, very alone. I don't really remember much more, I have a vision of the pre-op area and then coming round again in the same place.

I remember the voice in my head and starting to cry again, it was when the nurse was telling me it all went well and I had only been about 6-7 weeks pregnant, and the part of me was saying, you had more time, why didn't you wait. This pain is so unbearable, it is indescribable, I am actually feeling it now, my heart is breaking and my chest hurts, my eyes fill with tears. I don't know where it is coming from, I have never felt this pain before. Well I have, once before…

Maybe, this is what I am here for… Maybe to release this trapped person. Here I go with the maybes again. Maybe this is a lost soul part that needs retrieving, the lost diamond within in me.

This part of me was wailing this time, saying there had been enough time to wait and make the decision that was right.

But the decision had been made and it was all over. The next thing I remember was waking up in a room of beds and one by one people left. I didn't speak to any of them, I was just numb.

Nobody spoke to me. I remember just two things when I left I remember asking him to stop at the garage to collect my cigarettes from the day before, which they say they didn't have, and eating the meal he had prepared, or pushing it around my plate, but I don't remember what it was, I can guess it was a breaded or coated chicken piece with something as unhealthy on the side.

Elizabeth Goddard

Nothing more.
Did we watch TV?
Did I just go to bed?

I have no idea.

I was dead Inside.

Finding Lily

Elizabeth Goddard

Elizabeth Goddard

When you just
need to talk

A few days later, it could have been a week, I was ill, I woke up, my body burning and I fainted when I went to the toilet. I went to the doctors and was told I had an infection. I called my ex but he couldn't talk as he was out with someone from work. I don't remember anything more about this time.

I must have gone back to work on the Monday following the operation, maybe I took a few days holiday.

My son must have come home from Devon.
I must have been taking him to school, I just don't remember.

I was dead inside.

No one said anything. Did they see me withdraw from life? Perhaps I didn't, perhaps I put on a mask...

Finding Lily

Elizabeth Goddard

Elizabeth Goddard

Something Missing

Looking at this girl next to me, I realised I knew that feeling, I can see she is alive and breathing but something inside her had died.

Mine was an emptiness, a void. Something was missing. I wondered if my eyes had been like hers, hollow with no soul.

I wondered if anyone around me had noticed it.

No one said anything. Did they see me withdraw from life? Perhaps I didn't, perhaps I put on a mask...

I have no recollection of what was happening just a feeling of numbness. I can see that in her now.

And then, one evening someone handed me the biggest part of the puzzle or maybe a few pieces that all fitted together.

I don't really recall the feeling, anger? But, a part of me jumped in, an assertive me. I can still remember where I was sitting; I can still see the image across the bar of me just staring forward.

Finding Lily

Elizabeth Goddard

Elizabeth Goddard

Who turned the lights on?

It can't have been long after the abortion, I had been invited to a friend's flat warming party. I was at the wine bar after work on the Friday as usual. I remember being sat at a table talking to a friend; I was close to both her and her partner and had been for many years. It was her partner I was talking to just after my appointment on the 14th, he was the one who stopped her interrupting our conversation.

I have no idea why she was telling me this, but she was telling me about Valentines night.

I don't know what the conversation was leading up to this point.

I don't know if I asked her.

Finding Lily

She was telling me how she and her partner had been out with my ex and her.

I wonder what my thoughts were then in that moment.

I think I was stunned.

Was I surprised?

I don't really recall the feeling, anger? But, a part of me jumped in, an assertive me. I can still remember where I was sitting; I can still see the image across the bar of me just staring forward.

Mis-demeanour's isn't there now, quite funny really, as it means minor wrong doing... If it was still standing I could point out exactly where we were sitting, 2nd table back from the arch in the bar area.

Had they both spoken about this?
Had my friends decided I needed to know?

Was I making a fool out of myself still being with him in a un-relationship sort of way? Everyone else knowing that they were together but me.
I remember it being like an out of body experience, I remember staring towards the bar and then glancing back towards my friend, what I did notice in the brief moment was her go to the toilet, then a few seconds later he followed her.

Elizabeth Goddard

*My friend was still talking and saying something about a
napkin and maybe she did something, she was being loud,
maybe she threw water at him, or was it pushing off his chair,
it is irrelevant now.*

*After a while, she came back to the bar and so I headed to the
mens toilet, he was standing at urinal; bearing in mind she
had returned, I found that odd... And I do remember saying
something about it, probably sarcastic as that is my hurt
fallback character.*

*I challenged him and he marched off and left the bar. He
wouldn't acknowledge they were an item or in a relationship,
which is quite sad really. Not for me, but for her. He
probably thought I would say something or make a scene in
the bar and she and everyone would find out what had
happened weeks before.*

*I was still going to go to the party, everyone was leaving, I had
arranged a lift there and back.*

*After he left, I had another couple of drinks, more than I had
intended and decided I would leave my car at work. Someone
had offered me a lift home, but she insisted she would drop me
back home.*

Finding Lily

For all these years, I just thought she was going to give me a lift home; but maybe she was going to tell me about them. And only now, has that thought come to me.

They must have planned to meet up afterwards; they may have planned to stay over at the hotel they were meeting at, which they did that night, it is irrelevant now, back then it wouldn't have been.

Anyway, I will never know the reason for her giving me the lift, she said it was because of the person who had offered me the lift home; he had recently had a breakdown and she was concerned for my safety. Maybe that is the truth, I will never know because I asked her what was going on and during the five minute drive, I told her about the abortion. I don't know what I said or how I started it, and bearing in mind I had only just found out that they were possibly an item.

Looking back now I hadn't realised the pain she would have felt. It really never occurred to me what she would have to deal with.

She was being told that the guy she was in love with, had been unfaithful to her. I never thought of her, I was consumed in my own grief.
She and her partner (not my ex) had been having fertility treatment; and here I was, blurting out my hurt over having terminated a pregnancy.

Elizabeth Goddard

It was probably the last time I saw her for quite a few years...
12 if I think about it...

Before she left, she told me that if she had known I was
pregnant, she would have made him keep it. That hurt!
She drove off into the night, I thought she was driving 60
miles home, well she didn't, she drove to meet him, I know
they stayed in a hotel in Worplesdon, as a few months later
one of colleagues told me he saw them leaving the following
morning.
And I knew they had met because, when I went in to change,
I got a phone call from him, screaming at me for telling her...

So this was my fault... I can chuckle at that thought
now... But, maybe he was right!

When I think of my own soul plan, I've done 100s
for people, and I have done my own and had people
read it for me. Assertiveness is a big thing for me, I
need to be more assertive or I can be over
assertive... It is only now, that I can see that, well
maybe I have thought about it before, but going
over this I realise, like the incident in the bar, when a
friend had to stand up for me, I tend to take a step
back and fit in with my partner's needs.

The whole situation over the abortion; if I had been
more assertive I would have said, NO, I want this
baby, rather than step back hoping someone would

Finding Lily

step in and say, no don't be silly, are you sure you
want this?...
I wanted someone to step forward for me, just like
my friend, when the person who should have done it
was me.

A friend picked me up and I told her; looking back I
now wonder if her and her partner had known
something, why did she pick that night to tell me?

I went to the party with friends and then stayed on
their sofa.

Neither of us went home that night.

I have no idea what I would have done, and today I still don't know, but I wasn't given that chance.

Finding Lily

Elizabeth Goddard

Seeing the bigger picture

Over the next few days, the bits of the puzzle were starting to come together.

The boxer shorts that went missing the night of the Christmas party; he had told me he had soiled them and had to leave them in the public toilet.

There was a time I found another pair covered in blood; he said he needed to go to the doctors to find out what was going on.

The wedding, we had been invited as day guests, she had only been invited to the evening; the time it took for him to go back to our house and pick her up never worked out for me, he was gone for hours.

Elizabeth Goddard

Her always being around for exercise classes on the days he was training at the gym.

The night we all went out together, I know we had separated at this point and he had had to put her in the bath as she had been sick all over the sofa.

My sister phoning me up and saying she had seen them coming out of a coffee shop together during the day. Had she told me they were holding hands? Can't recall now, I just said they were friends.

All the Fridays she had been staying

There are so many more…

Where the pain for me was so deep, was deceit, after all it was me who finished our relationship in the September, to his relief I might add. He was a free agent, but not telling me he was seeing someone else, allowing me to think there was a chance of us getting back together.

But I don't think it was just the two of us, me and her I mean. When we did get back together, I remember him telling me he went out on a date with a colleague's ex-girlfriend. But the biggest emotional pain for me, was not having the time to make a decision over my baby. I have no idea what I would have done, and today I still don't know, but I wasn't given that chance.

Finding Lily

I wasn't assertive enough to say no, this is my body, my decision. I was weak and broken. I remember the pain I was in, and it went on forever.

Some of the final pieces were given to me a few months later.

So, after staying on a friends sofa and climbing into bed with them in the morning like a small child seeking support from her parents, I got a lift back to my car. When I got home I realised he hadn't been home either.

When we finally were both back home, I have no idea what happened. I don't know if he just came in and ignored me. I don't know if we spoke about it, but I do remember during the next week, one night I opened his brandy and drank a lot of it.

He wasn't happy, understandably; he didn't understand what I was going through. I don't know if he did or didn't want to, because it would mean facing up to what he had done.

I had hardly told anyone at this point, if you have to hide things from people then that is wrong.

Finding Lily

Elizabeth Goddard

The Pain

When he finally came back from where ever he had been, I tried to tell him about my pain. I remember this quite clearly, he blanked me and went to bed, so I wrote it down, he ignored it so I tore it up. I was drunk, but I knew exactly what I was saying and doing,

That was the moment I made the decision to leave.

I called work the next day told my boss that I needed to move out and needed the day off and he agreed, so I packed up our lives, mine and my sons, in black bin bags threw them in to the back of the car and went to stay at my dad's.

That should have been the end really, most normal people would have said enough is enough, I'm done. Well, to a point I did. I joined the gym, started going out with girlfriends again.

Elizabeth Goddard

I was starting to deal with the pain of the last 6 months, probably longer. I told another really old friend of mine what had been happening,

I had hardly told anyone at this point, if you have to hide things from people then that is wrong. What was it, the fear that they would be honest and I was desperately trying to hang on to a relationship and a person that was clearly wrong for me?
Was it a fear of something?
Yes it was. But why?

Today I can see more clearly, but it has taken me 26 years to get to this point!

We were still working together and we were still in contact. He was starting to come round at the weekend. I remember him saying he had been to the hospital with her and something about it, I don't know now. I don't ever think we really spoke about what happened properly.

He must have still been seeing her, I don't know, but then I didn't care.
I remember him coming over one evening and was talking about doing something, I told him I couldn't as I had a date, he told me that if I went out with this guy any chance of us getting together would be over.

Finding Lily

And what a plonker I was. I was rebuilding my life, I was getting stronger every day, yet here I was cancelling the date! As it turned out, when I met this guy again 12 years later, he was the same person my ex was, out of the frying pan in to the fire my grandmother would have said.

I question now why I was doing this, was it for the security of having a house?
A relationship?

One of my friends was having a ball at the time, she was dating a few different people, I should have been doing that, but I didn't, the unassertive me said 'Oh Ok' and cancelled the date.

Over a few months we sort of started dating again, nothing said we sort of fell in to it.

Perhaps it did start in the November, but he forgot to say which year.

Finding Lily

Elizabeth Goddard

The Napkin

When I look around again the young girl has taken her hair down. She does look familiar now, her long think wavy hair and stunning dark eyes. She looks more present than before, relaxed and beautiful. I have seen her somewhere before.

It all fell in to place.

I remember the evening, we went to Portsmouth, it was cold and dark, he was playing football so I went to sit in the car. Bored, I opened the glove compartment and there in front of me was a pile of 'stuff'. One of the items was a napkin with 14 months together or something like that written on it, 'the napkin' I had been told about.

I was so shocked at finding this had been going on for 14 months...

He told me it had started in the November and only a few months earlier, which worked time wise as we

had split up in the September, and now I remember
my friend telling me about the napkin.

Wow 26 years later the bits are still fitting together...

Perhaps it did start in the November, but he forgot
to say which year.

So maybe it started before the Christmas party, it
really doesn't matter now.

Each little event is like opening a wound over and over again. It is like taking off a plaster a little bit at a time.

Finding Lily

Elizabeth Goddard

Elizabeth Goddard

Being Cracked Open

I remember the anger, I couldn't tell him on the drive back, as we had given someone a lift. I do remember going back to his house and I think I was going to stay over. I remember his reaction when I challenged him, it was to punch the kitchen door, to the side of my head. That was it for me; I went to leave, and then the begging started. He begged me to stay.

I just don't get why he thought it was easier to hide it all rather than get it all out in the open.

Each little event is like opening a wound over and over again. It is like taking off a plaster a little bit at a time.

I remember people saying to me that they thought I had known. If they had known and thought we had split up, why not saying anything?

Finding Lily

Why not talk about it? Or, were they asked not to?
So not to hurt my feelings.

That pain and fear is still there...

Finding Lily

Elizabeth Goddard

Trust

We did end up back together, but in truth, the trust was gone, and our relationship was built on weak foundations. I often wondered if it was the need to be whole that led me to get back together or the competitive side of me, the need to win.

That pain and fear was still there...

And the ability never to be able to discuss what happened didn't help in that process either.
At the end of the year, I decided the time was right to finish it. But, he bought me a leather jacket for Christmas, rather than say thank you but it is over, I can't accept this, I remember thinking, I can get him something for his birthday in a few weeks and then I can finish it.

It didn't happen, shortly after his birthday, I found out I was pregnant.

Elizabeth Goddard

I remember reading an article on affairs, and how women who stay with their men, only usually hang round for a year. I think it was around the time Hugh Grant had been caught in the back of a car with a prostitute, and Liz Hurley stood by him for a year and then that finished.

He had left the company we worked for in the early summer of the year before and ironically he went to the company she worked for. I pretended not to have an issue with it.
I then left in the October to work for a big corporation and was doing really well.

So, it was mid to late March, nearly a month after his birthday and I hadn't got round to finishing the relationship. I felt odd and did a test and I was pregnant.

Where most people would have felt joy, I remember thinking I am not going through that again. I went over and over again the emotions I had felt; again how wrong it had been, and now I was pregnant again with him, but the worst bit for me, and even now, is that I would have had the first one in September and could easily had the next one.

Finding Lily

I have thought about this for years, over and over in my head and I still do...

I told him, the assertive me; that I wasn't going that again!

I have gone over and over, using the excuse that I may not have had my girls. But I could have!

That still eats away at me.

It's

a

journey

Finding Lily

Elizabeth Goddard

Life goes on

Life goes on, it is a journey, 16 months following the birth of my daughter, I had a second.

I didn't have as many negative emotions around this pregnancy, but it did bring up some.

"And this is what I learned: You can be shattered and then you can put yourself back together piece by piece.

But what can happen over time is this: You wake up one day and realise that you have put yourself back together completely differently."

-Glennon Doyle Melton

Finding Lily

Elizabeth Goddard

But it never ends

Our relationship finally broke down nine years later, we had had some good times and two beautiful daughters, but there was always a shadow hovering over it.

Unspoken.

Perhaps if he could even acknowledge what had happened, what I went through and why, because for me that was the biggie. We needed to build strong foundations for our relationship but it didn't happen.

To put someone through that to protect yourself.

I remember reading an article about the effect abortion has on women, how they never forget that life changing experience. It is so true,

Elizabeth Goddard

It reminds me of a blog I have recently read from Glennon Doyle Melton - She said

"And this is what I learned: You can be shattered and then you can put yourself back together piece by piece.
But what can happen over time is this: You wake up one day and realize that you have put yourself back together completely differently."

This is what happened for me, I think. As I healed I went back together differently.

I'm not going to use the
word 'normal' because
I hate the word,
what is normal?

Finding Lily

Elizabeth Goddard

I do know her

I glance to the side again; I know where I know her from!

We met 4 years ago on a course.

After the birth of my first daughter, I realised something wasn't quite right. I couldn't put her down, she never slept, but working and being ill then falling pregnant so quickly again, I got used to it, just like the stain on your carpet you keep meaning to clean and you walk over and over it until you don't notice it anymore. When my second daughter was born she was a joy she slept like a baby, I now had evidence that this wasn't, I'm going to use the word 'normal' yuk, because I hate the word, what is normal?

Finding Lily

This was the start of my journey along the holistic route. It turns out she had suffered with birth trauma and that is why she was unhappy and didn't sleep.

I had been working full-time but something inside me was calling me. I retrained, I may have got there on my own, but I think what happened looking to help her was in fact helping me.

It was totally unexpected.
The pain had mellowed over
the years; it had been slowly
pushed to one side.

Finding Lily

Elizabeth Goddard

Her name is Lily!

I knew, I knew her...

In 2011, I decided I would like to retrain as a spiritual life coach and part of the course included becoming a Soul Plan Practitioner.

There I met Roger, well actually, we met via Facebook; he was doing a talk on Soul Plans before I did the training and I wanted to find out more. When I arrived to do my training he was on the course as well; he was training to become a trainer.

The following year, I was interested in the course he was running called psychic art.

It was April 2012, and I didn't really know what to expect.

Nor was prepared for what was about to happen.

Elizabeth Goddard

We were shown a clearing technique which I found
so powerful and now, use it with some clients.
Through art you clear away emotions and trauma.

On the Saturday, the part of me that I only thought
of now on Valentine's day and an odd few occasions
came to the surface.

It was totally unexpected. The pain had mellowed
over the years; it had been slowly pushed to one
side.

So here it was. I could feel the emotion all over
again.
The hurt, the anger and the guilt.

I was in total shock that this would come up to the
surface!

This was what I needed to heal, at this moment, to
move on.

As I felt the pain again, I remember colouring a red
heart on the page; and as I went deeper in to the
emotion it disappeared under a veil of blackness -
that void I had felt.

There was not a trace of red left on the page.

Finding Lily

It was my baby and then the pain. I needed to set
fire to it and release the emotion.

On the Sunday, I returned to the workshop and we
worked on drawing spirit guides.
Roger demonstrated psychic art and connected with
a guide for the group.

Her name was Lily…

When he finished I was in shock, she was the image
of my younger daughter. She was stunning and
beautiful, with long flowing wavy hair. She was there
for the group, but she also was connecting with each
of us individually and for me it was allowing me to
let go.

I did this and she forgave me, she told me it was
OK, but now, I realise, I never let go of the months
and years and I never healed myself around that
time!

I have done a lot of healing around her, the decision
I made or didn't make; because by not making a
decision is making one.

And, in shock at the lengths people will go to in
order to protect themselves, the stories and lies or

half truths it was is shocking not to be seen as a bad person.

I can't believe this has just happened!

I am feeling inside for the pain I had been feeling when I think about the situation again and I can't feel anything.

Finding Lily

Elizabeth Goddard

Elizabeth Goddard

Like an Angel

Seeing Lily again today, sitting next to her, going back into that pain and releasing the hurt has helped me.

I did need the space to clear my head. I was drawn here for a reason and it was to connect with her again.

Not for me to help her, but the other way round once again!

I looked around to her again, and she has finished her drink, she is getting ready to leave and she blows me a kiss as she walks away, the image of an angel.

I can't believe this has just happened!

Finding Lily

I am feeling inside for the pain I had been feeling, the pain I felt about the situation and I can't feel anything. The anguish has gone. The guilt has gone.

We are multi-faceted beings, our lives are multi-faceted as well, finding the diamond inside of me is what I have been looking for...

I am ready to move on!

I have once again put myself back together; I just need to find out who I have now become...

Elizabeth Goddard

Finding Lily

Dear reader,

As I said at the beginning of this book, this is how I remember the events, this is my version; if you were to speak to the people involved they will have a different story. They may not even remember this happening.

If this has affected you in anyway please speak to someone, turn your pain around in to a positive experience. You don't have to relive any of it there are ways to releasing pain and trauma effectively, and this is how I help clients.

I have added the Ho'oponopo below to help with forgiveness and after that, a script to help with limiting beliefs.

If you don't need them that is fine.

Liz Goddard

Elizabeth Goddard

"I am sorry"
"Please forgive me"
"Thank you"
"I love you"

Ho'oponopono is a very ancient Hawaiian art of problem solving. as a gift to be shared and practiced.

Mornah Simeona is recognised for updating and bringing it forward she was healer in Hawaii and taught her updated version of ho'oponopono throughout the United States, Asia and Europe.

Ho'oponopono means to make right or to rectify an error.

"We are the sum total of our experiences, which is to say that we are burdened by our pasts. When we experience stress or fear in our lives, if we would look carefully, we would find that the cause is actually a memory. It is the emotions which are tied to these memories which affect us now. The subconscious associates an action or person in the present with something that happened in the past. When this occurs, emotions are activated and stress is produced."

By saying these words over and over, a person is said to connect her/his own inner light with the light of Source. Over time, patterns in the subconscious dissolve, and by forgiving the parts within that hold those patterns, the person's outer world regains balance and harmony.

Finding Lily

This Script by Karol Trueman is designed to help move limiting beliefs.

Follow your intuition as far as how frequently you need to say this, and use it as often as you like on as many issues as you like. Make note of any shifts in your life in response to this commitment.

Spirit/Super-Conscious, please locate the origin of my feeling(s)/thought(s) of _____. Take each and every level, layer, area, and aspect of my Being to this origin. Analyse and resolve it perfectly with God's truth. Come through all generations of time and eternity, healing every incident and its appendages based on the origin.
Please do it according to God's will until I'm at the present – filled with light and truth, God's peace and love, forgiveness of myself for my incorrect perceptions, forgiveness of every person, place, circumstance, and event which contributed to this/these feeling(s)/thought(s). With total forgiveness and unconditional love, I allow every physical, mental, emotional, and spiritual problem and inappropriate behaviour based on the negative origin recorded in my DNA, to transform. I choose being_____. I feel_____. I AM_____. (Basically, use the same appropriate positive feeling(s) for each blank line, to replace the negative feeling(s).)

It is done. It is healed. It is accomplished Now!

Elizabeth Goddard

Lily Channelled by Roger Hanson

Finding Lily

Elizabeth Goddard

About the Author

Liz Goddard is a Soul Purpose Coach working with women internationally at that #fuckthis moment in their lives…

She offers a coaching programme - Soul Purpose and runs retreats in Greece to help women heal and share their own stories for the greater good.

Her compassion and way of working helps people connect with who they really are and the message they have to share with the world around them. Her passion is working through the trauma without reliving it… She never asks of her clients something she isn't prepared to deal with herself.

Liz has a passion for being creative, in life, in business, in healing. She loves to travel and discover places of healing and would love to share them with you…

If you would like to find out how to work with her you can visit her website
reviveyoursoul.co.uk

Finding Lily

This is the story of
Love
Loss
Trauma
Healing
and Forgiveness

This is the story of finding the Diamond

Elizabeth Goddard

Finding Lily